Daddy Is a Doodlebug

Daddy Is a Doodlebug

BRUCE DEGEN

HarperCollins Publishers

To achieve crispness and clarity in the black line artwork,

each illustration was prepared in two stages: the black pen-and-ink

overlay was executed on Strathmore Bristol paper and the color

artwork was executed in gouache on separate sheets.

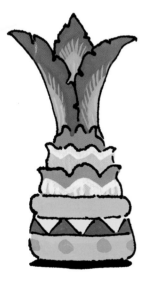

Daddy Is a Doodlebug
Copyright © 2000 by Bruce Degen. Printed in the U.S.A. All rights reserved.
http://www.harperchildrens.com
Library of Congress Cataloging-in-Publication Data
Degen, Bruce.
    Daddy is a doodlebug / Bruce Degen.
        p.   cm.
    Summary: A young doodlebug describes how he and his father are alike and the things they
enjoy doing together.
    ISBN 0-06-028415-3. — ISBN 0-06-028416-1 (lib. bdg.)
    [1.Fathers and sons—Fiction.   2. Insects—Fiction.   3. Stories in rhyme.]
I. Title.
PZ8.3.D364Dad   2000   98-49563
[E]—dc21   CIP
                                                                                              AC
Typography by Matt Adamec   1   2   3   4   5   6   7   8   9   10   ❖   First Edition

For Benoodle and Sandoodle

Daddy is a doodlebug.
I'm a doodlebug too.

We doodle things together
That doodlebugs like to do.

We are soup-with-noodle bugs,
We are apple strudel bugs,

We both eat potoodle chips
While walking through the zoo.
'Cause Daddy is a foodlebug,
And I'm a foodlebug too.

We walk our poodlebug down the lane,

We ride the caboodle car on the train,

We padoodle the canoe in the sun and rain.
That's what doodlebugs do.

'Cause Daddy is a canoedlebug,
And I'm a canoedlebug too.

We go for bugoodle rides in the park,

We count the firefloodles when they spark,

We play hoodle and seekbug in the dark—
Find me and I'll find you!

'Cause Daddy is a tagoodlebug,
And I'm a tagoodlebug too.

We read together in our chair
Fairytoodles we like to share—

"Goldiebug and the Three Woolly Bears,"

"Robin Hoodlebug" too.

'Cause Daddy is a storyoodlebug,
And I'm a storyoodlebug too.

At night when we turn out the light,
We say, "Snug as a bug!
Don't let the bedboodles bite!
Sweet bug dreams and goodlebug night."

That's what doodlebugs do.

'Cause Daddy is a doodlebug,

And I'm a doodlebug too.